A GIFT FOR:

Aileen – Happy Easter 2016!

FROM:

Love, Donna ☺

Copyright © 2015 Hallmark Licensing, LLC

Published by Hallmark Gift Books,
a division of Hallmark Cards, Inc.,
Kansas City, MO 64141
Visit us on the Web at Hallmark.com.

Editorial Director: Carrie Bolin
Editor: Kim Schworm Acosta
Art Director: Jan Mastin
Designer: Scott Swanson
Production Designer: Dan Horton

ISBN: 978-1-59530-841-2
BOK2196

Printed and bound in China
DEC14

Mimi

FINDS HER SONG

By Bill Gray

Illustrated by Ramon Olivera

Hallmark

In a beautiful, downtown concert hall,
there's a tiny gap, way up in the wall.
And as singers sing their songs below,
Mimi, a mouse, watches every show.

Mimi loves music of any old kind—
country or rock, she doesn't mind.
Whether an opera or a new hip-hop song,
Mimi will listen and then sing along.

Sometimes it's her favorite—a pretty pop star,
who sings as she strums on a bright, pink guitar.
And as Mimi sings with her, she knows this is true:
One day, on a stage, she will be a star, too.

Mimi's family lives in the attic together—
brothers and sisters and cousins, whomever.
And each time a show far below is all through,
Mimi sings all of the songs for them, too!

So after each show, with a broomstick guitar,
her stage is a shoebox, and she is the star.
Her family applauds—then her mom stops the show.
"No encores, Mimi. It's bedtime, you know."

Mimi's dad tucks her into her matchbox bed tight
and then gently kisses her forehead good night.
And as each of her sisters snuggles into her mitten,
she sings them the lullaby that she had written.

Now, one day at Mouse School, Mimi's friend Ann
came running up to her with a sheet in her hand.
"Talent show, Mimi!" Ann squeaked, all delighted.
And as Mimi read, she was clearly excited.

"I'll write a great song!" Mimi said over dinner.
And her cousin Jacob said, "You'll be the winner!"
Homework and dishes were done before long,
then Mimi got comfy to write her great song.

She thought and she thought as she chewed on her pen.
Then she crossed it all out and began it again.
"You could write about cheese," brother Michael advised.
"Gouda or cheddar!" Mimi just rolled her eyes.

"I know just the thing!" said a cousin named Gary,
"You could write about cats! Make your song real scary!"
Her smart sister Bella looked up from her reading.
"A song about science might be just what you're needing!"

Mimi was grateful for all their suggestions,
but to sing about those things was out of the question.
Her song must be special! Important! First-rate!
Her song simply had to be perfectly great!

But bedtime was coming, the day nearly done.
Her song wasn't finished, not even begun.
That's when her grandfather held out his hand,
"Come with me, Mimi. I have a plan."

Mimi's mama came with them, and so, very soon,
they were walking through hallways lit up by the moon.
Mimi thought that she knew that old theater quite well,
but where they were going, she just couldn't tell.

They rounded a corner, climbed under a chair.
The three of them stopped, and Mimi just stared.
There was the stage she had dreamed of so long,
And her Grandpa said, "Go, Mimi! Go find your song!"

Mimi walked on the stage, up close to the edge,
and imagined an audience out past the ledge.
The stars, through a window, were twinkling their light,
and Mimi felt just like a star that night.

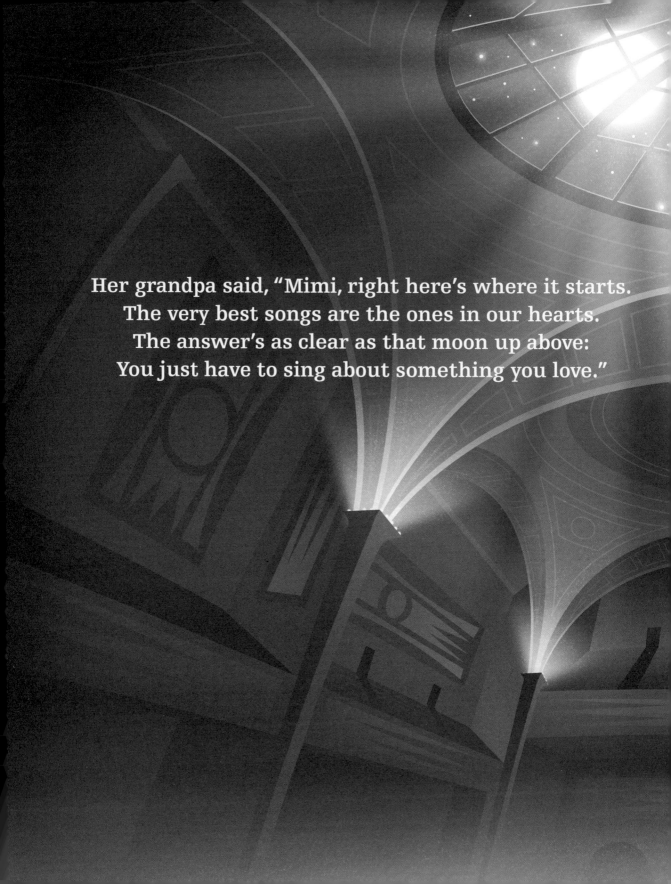

Her grandpa said, "Mimi, right here's where it starts.
The very best songs are the ones in our hearts.
The answer's as clear as that moon up above:
You just have to sing about something you love."

The next day in school when the talent show came,
the teacher stood up, and she said Mimi's name.
And when Mimi reached this line in her song,
"Let's all sing together," they all sang along!

Next night, at the theater, a band rocked the hall,
as Mimi smiled down through her hole in the wall.
Then she turned in, after good nights were said,
and the talent show trophy stood next to her bed.

Did you have fun with Mim
We would love to hear from you

Please send your comments t
Hallmark Book Feedbac
P.O. Box 41903
Mail Drop 10
Kansas City, MO 6414

Or e-mail us a
booknotes@hallmark.co

For more fun, visit Hallmark.com/Mimi.